Book One

A CHRISTMAS SURPRISE

The Littlest Kaiju Series

Jason Cordova

Publisher's Note: This is a work of fiction. Names, characters, places, and incidents are a product of the author's vivid and over-active imagination. I mean, can you imagine what would happen if a ten-year-old girl *actually* received a kaiju for Christmas? The chaos would be incredible and probably very bad. We've all seen the movies and we can all agree that this never ends well for most people. Cities smashed, lots of damage… it's hard to explain away a destroyed skyscraper. Locales and public names are sometimes used for atmospheric purposes. Any resemblance to actual people or kaiju, living or dead, or to any business companies, events, institutions, or locations is completed coincidental. Especially events which may or may not have occurred in the Arctic Circle.

Cover Art & Design: **Emily Mottesheard** www.mottfolio.com

For more of the author's work, please visit www.jasoncordova.com

Acknowledgments

This book wouldn't have been possible without the loving support of my friends and family. It's a really long list. Thanks in particular goes out to Emily Motteshead from Mottfolio Design for the baby kaiju picture which started it all.

CHAPTER 1 – THE SURPRISE

For three hundred and twenty-three days Kyra Wachtel was the ideal ten year old girl. She completed her chores, kept her grades up in school (well, she was struggling with history, but Kyra always thought history was very boring), and was a good older sister to her younger brothers, Aiden and Jayden, aka the twins of terror. The missing seventeen days didn't count in her book, since they were all in the summer and everyone knew that Santa didn't count the naughty days

that happened in July.

All her planning led to Christmas Eve. Every year she and her brothers could open one present before bed. The only downside was that her parents got to pick the present. Still, an early present was far better than nothing at all. The best part was that after everyone would go to bed, she could stay up as late as she wanted to play with her new toy. As long as she stayed quiet, at least. One year she had forgotten to turn the volume down on her new mp3 player after sneaking it to her room, and had it connected to her mother's speaker system downstairs. That had not gone over well with her parents.

As her mother brought out the presents, Kyra could barely keep her excitement contained. All she wanted was a dog. Well, at the top of the list was a dog. A very specific small dog, one that could sit on her lap and not squish her. The list to Santa had a few other items, like a new sweater and basketball shoes. At the top, underlined twice and written in all caps, was DOG. Not a puppy, either. Her brothers had Romeo, a pudgy bulldog, since he was a puppy. She remembered just how many times the twins had to take the Romeo out when he had been young and did not want to do that. Because of this, and the many times she had been forced to clean up puddles on the kitchen floor because the twins weren't home, she had purposely written DOG.

Kyra's eyes widened as her mother carried in a large box. While not big enough to carry a full-grown dog like a boxer, there was more than enough space for a Shih Tzu or something similar in size. Her excitement began to grow as something inside the box moved.

"Oof! This thing is heavy!" her mother exclaimed. Kyra could barely contain herself. She giggled and bounced up and down on the couch. There could be only one thing in the box, and all of Kyra's hard work and planning were about to pay off. He mother scolded her. "Settle down, Kyra. Don't make him nervous."

"Sorry," Kyra replied and tucked her hands under her legs. Her smile grew wider. The excitement was almost overwhelming and it took everything in her power not to jump up and snatch the box from her mother's hands.

"Jayden, Aiden, you two open your

presents first," Kyra's father told them. Kyra nearly whined as she had to wait as the boys unwrapped their presents. The *oohs* and *ahhs* nearly pushed her impatience over the edge. The boys had received identical handheld tablets, the difference being in color only. One blue, and one red. Jayden, whose favorite color was red, had already flopped onto his stomach on the ground and turned his new device on. Aiden was scrambling around trying to find a wall plug so he could charge his, since he figured that the battery would be close to dying and Kyra knew that he would want to play with his new device.

"Thanks Mom, Dad!" the boys chorused simultaneously.

"Thank Santa, you mean," came the reply from their father.

"Dad, Santa comes tonight," Jayden replied as he fiddled with his device.

"The mail still works," their mother countered. "He could have had it express delivered, you know."

"Oh. Okay," Aiden said as he finally turned his device on. "That works too."

"All right Kyra, time for you to open yours," her mother said as she set the box before her. Whatever was on the inside had obviously settled down by now and Kyra, no longer able to control herself, lunged for it.

"Oh wow, oh wow," she breathed as she picked the box up and put it on her lap. It was heavy, and she could see a set of air holes in the back. A giant ribbon with a bow decorated the top. Fortunately, there was no wrapping paper for her to dispose of. Kyra looked at her mother, who motioned for the young girl to remove the lid of the box. Grabbing the lid with her fingertips, she pulled it off and tossed it aside. She peered inside and suddenly screamed as a decidedly non-furry face popped out of the box. She pushed the box off her legs and onto the cushion next to her. Scrambling back on to the arm rest of the couch, she pointed at the box. "What is that?!"

Inside the box was definitely *not* a dog. It was dark red in color and covered in scales. On the head were three horns, one where each ear was supposed to be, and another on his forehead. Kyra blinked as she recognized another horn on his snout. It looked more like a crocodile than anything else, though it wasn't like anything she had seen on television. Two big eyes were staring back at her, shining in the bright light. It was a little on the chubby side, which made it look like a big fat scaly baby. *With horns and a beak*, Kyra thought. She could see a short, stumpy tail thumping against the side of the box and felt the solid blows on her hand.

"Bill, what *is* that thing?" Kyra's mother stopped and stared as well. The sudden noise drew the attention of the boys as well, who both popped their heads up to see.

"I... uh, I don't know," Kyra's father admitted as he took his glasses off and cleaned them with his shirt. He put them back onto his nose and squinted. "That's no dog. Anjelica, where did the pug go?"

"That *thing* ate my dog?!" Kyra shrieked. The beast in the box yowled back and poked its head out of the box. It made a noise and seemed to smile at them. The eyes grew wider as it inspected the room around. It chirped once before it began to make a very unsettling cooing sound. Kyra shook her head. "No. I don't care. Santa messed up. That is *not* a dog!"

"Well, it seems friendly enough," her father allowed as he reached out. The creature half-closed its eyes and made an odd rumbling sound as he began to pet the creature. "I think- I think it's *purring*."

"Dog's don't purr," Kyra said and, using her legs, gingerly pushed the box to the other end of the sofa. The creature's head moved and watched her the entire time. She wanted it as far away from her as possible.

In this history of big mistakes, this one obviously took the cake. Santa had messed up somewhere, Kyra was certain. She wanted a dog and this was *not* a dog. In fact, she didn't even know what it was.

"Aw, he's cute," Jayden said. "Santa got you a pet kaiju! Can I keep him? You can have my tablet, sis. Please?"

"No, you can have mine!" Aiden countered. "Dad, can we trade with Kyra?"

"Hold on one second," their father shook his head. "There's been some kind of mistake here."

"Wait," Kyra said and moved to the box. The creature inside mewled at her and two arms popped out of the top of the box. To Kyra it appeared to be asking her to be picked up. She shook off the feeling. "What's a kaiju?"

"A monster!" the boys chimed in. Kyra's mother frowned.

"No, boys. Kaiju is just the Japanese word for 'strange creature'," she corrected the boys. She looked at her husband. "Bill, we can't keep it. We have to turn it in to the pound or something."

"It's eight o'clock at night on Christmas Eve, dear," he said as he checked his phone. "There's no way anybody is open tonight. We have an old crate we can put the kaiju thing in until the vet is open in two days. Then we can figure out what's going on, and what happened to the pug."

"So how do you propose we get it in the crate, mister?" Kyra's mom asked.

"I'll do it," Kyra said and, before her parents could react, scooped up the baby kaiju into her arms. The scales, while looking shiny, seemed to radiate a mild heat. Her friend at school had a bearded dragon and the kaiju, while possessing many of the same features, acted like it was warm-blooded. The creature pressed the top of its head into Kyra's chest and continued to make its strange rumbling purr sound. She winced as the horn in top of his head poked her. "Ow."

"Did he bite you?" her father asked, concerned.

"No," Kyra answered as she looked down at the small creature. Those bright luminescent eyes were finally closed and not locked onto her. It was weird, but for a brief instance she had a feeling that the baby kaiju had recognized her somehow. "His horn poked me. The one on his forehead, not the, uh, ears or nose?"

"Well, put him in the crate before he does bite someone," Kyra's mother insisted. Kyra nodded and, her arms full of the tiny kaiju, carefully walked back to the mud room near the rear of the house.

The kaiju was surprisingly calm throughout the short trip, his head still pressed firmly in the middle of her chest. It cooed and seemed content, which was weird. She'd seen the movies and wondered if this kaiju was like the city destroying, people-eating monsters. It certainly wasn't acting like it. Maybe it needed to grow up a bit more before it would go eat a city? Kyra had no clue.

The kaiju started to make more noise as she struggled to get the crate open. It was an older dog crate but was still in relatively good shape, considering. Squawking loudly, it tried to grab onto her shirt with its claws but Kyra wasn't having any of that. She patiently removed each claw as the kaiju tried to cling to her until finally she was free. Moving quickly, she slipped the kaiju into the crate and closed the gate. She double-checked the water bowl inside the crate before she was satisfied.

"I have no idea what you eat, so hopefully you're not hungry," she muttered. A small bag on top of the dryer across from the crate caught her eye. It was one of the twin's bag of beef jerky. She smiled. "Even Romeo likes jerky, so you have to be able to eat it, too."

She snagged the bag and opened it up. It was still pretty full of jerky. Grabbing a few of the larger pieces, she began to tear them into smaller bite-sized pieces for the kaiju. Gingerly she pushed one of the smaller pieces of jerky through the side of the crate. The kaiju happily snapped them out of her hand.

"Hey!" she said. "Careful."

"Mrawp," the kaiju burped back and held out its claw for more. Kyra blinked, confused.

"You want more?" she asked it, not believing what was going on. It was as if the small creature could understand her.

"Mrawp!"

"Ooooooooooh kay," she drew out the word and passed more pieces of jerky through the crate. It took it from her fingers and happily began to gnaw on the tough dried meat. Amused, Kyra continued to slide hunks of dehydrated meat into the kaiju's waiting claw until the bag was empty. "Uh oh. No more."

"Mrawp?"

"No," she said. "No more. Time for bed for you, mister."

"Mrawp!"

"Don't argue with me," she said before stopping and slapping her forehead. Kyra couldn't believe the situation she was in. "I'm arguing with a tiny little monster. This is too strange. My life is weird."

"Mrawp." The kaiju seemed to agree with her.

"Good night little guy," she muttered as she walked out of the mud room, turning the light off as she left. Closing the door behind her, she looked at the empty bag of jerky still in her hand. "Oh great. One of the boys is going to be mad at me."

"Kyra?" she heard her mom call from the living room. "Everything okay?"

"Yeah mom," she answered back. Kyra tossed the empty bag into the recycling bin and hurried back into the living room. "I didn't know what to feed it, so I gave it some of the jerky I found back here."

"Hey!" Jayden yelled at her, looking up from his tablet. "That was mine!"

"Kyra Marie, did you eat your brother's jerky?" her mother asked loudly.

"No," she said. "I gave it to the kaiju.

"Kyra, you should have asked first," her mother admonished.

"Well, he was hungry," Kyra replied, her tone sulky. "I'll buy him another one."

"That's not the point," her father told her. "You throw a fit when your brothers touch your things, even when they promise to put it back. It'd be rather hypocritical of you to ignore their complaints, Kyra."

"Dad, you don't understand," Kyra tried to explain. "We can't feed that *thing* back there dog food! I was lucky it even bothered with the jerky!"

"Kyra, don't argue," her mother warned. "I appreciate your concern for the creature, but I seriously doubt that it would starve by breakfast. I can see if it likes raw eggs and steak, like Romeo, in the morning when I feed the dog. You could have waited and asked."

"Mom..." Kyra sighed. "You're right. I'm sorry."

"I would have said yes anyway," Jayden muttered in a sullen voice.

"I'm sorry Jayden," Kyra told her brother.

"Finally. I'm not getting blamed

for anything," Aiden chimed in.

"Aiden Michael, do you really want to go there?" their father asked.

"And there went that moment," Aiden muttered.

"Okay, seems like everyone is a little grumpy or too sarcastic for my tastes tonight," Kyra's father said as he got up out of his recliner. He stretched his back out before looking at his gathered children. "Time for bed."

"It's too early!" the twins whined simultaneously. "We have half an hour!"

"We can go to bed even earlier tomorrow night if you'd like," their father warned.

"Off to bed we go," Jayden announced and ran up the stairs to the twin's room, Aiden hot on his heels. At the top of the stairs Aiden stopped and called back down. "Night, love you!"

"Kyra? Will you plug the boy's tablets into the charger in the kitchen with yours before you go to bed?" her mother asked.

"Okay," Kyra replied and grabbed the tablets. After plugging them into the wall socket and coming back in the living, she looked at her mom and dad. "What are we going to do about the thing in the crate?"

"We'll talk more about it in the morning," her mother replied. "It's time for bed young lady."

"How did that thing get in my present?" Kyra continued. "What happened to the pug you were talking about?"

"No more, Kyra," her mother said in a stern tone. "I love you. Good night."

"Love you too. Night," Kyra replied back as she trudged up the stairs to her room.

CHAPTER 2 – A BRILLIANT PLAN

As Kyra lay in her bed, she couldn't help but think of all the things that could have happened. Had her parents played a cruel prank on her and replaced her dog with the kaiju? Had Santa made a huge mistake and somehow sent her a monster on accident? Where was the dog? Most importantly, how could she clear everything up with Santa so she could get rid of the baby kaiju. And, if she were very lucky, find the dog that she was supposed to have.

But how? That was the main question. She knew from a quick search online she had done before going to bed that the local animal shelter would stay closed until the day after Christmas, though there was the minor issue that she had never heard of anyone accepting a kaiju. Even if it were a baby.

Where had the creature come from? It was obvious from the way her parents reacted to the creature that they hadn't known he was in the box. So where did the dog go? How did they get it into the box if they hadn't known about the baby kaiju in the first place? There were a lot of unanswered questions that bothered Kyra, and there was almost no way she could find out.

Unless… Santa was behind all of this.

She thought about the song for a minute. Santa knew who had been bad or good, naughty and nice. Did those seventeen days in July really hurt her chances? No, she quickly decided. What happens at summer camp never counts because of rules and camp counselors. Whatever else was going on was something else. All of this she chalked up to Santa having some sort of magical ability to see things. But what if Santa's magic extended further out? Santa could help, but how could she ask him? There was no way the mail would arrive at the North Pole in time for him to help with the baby kaiju, especially on Christmas Eve. Kyra figured that Santa was probably already delivering presents in London and would be making his way across the Atlantic Ocean by now. If she wanted Santa's help in fixing this, she would have to talk to him when he showed up.

"That's it," she whispered as a plan began to form in the back of her mind. She would trap Santa and force him to take the kaiju! Even if it meant that her plan might get her onto the naughty list, it was worth the risk. She couldn't keep a kaiju around the house. What if it got out and ran around the neighborhood? Old Mrs. McNealty across the street was always calling her parents and tattling on her whenever she and her brothers were playing too loudly. She could only imagine what the elderly woman would do if she saw Kyra outside with a baby monster.

No, she would have to trap Santa. But how? That was a problem, because so far as she could tell, nobody had ever managed that before. She hadn't ever seen a video online with proof either. Well, not any which were very good, Kyra silently amended as she tossed and turned in bed. There were some halfway-decent fakes out there that had fooled some of her friends. Kyra, on the other hand, remained convinced that Santa was far sneakier and trickier than most gave someone his size credit for.

Still, she needed ideas. The best place for weird and off-the-wall stuff was on the internet. This meant breaking the rules, something she didn't really want to do on Christmas Eve. The naughty list was one place she did not want to end up on now. Not so close to Christmas.

Even though it was well past her lights out time, it was barely past ten.

She knew that her parents had already gone to bed. Her brothers would be asleep as well, which meant she had a few hours to prepare for Santa's arrival without being caught. Hopefully. With all this in mind, she quickly got out of bed and pulled her socks on. It was a little chilly downstairs, so she grabbed her robe as well.

There were three stairs which squeaked loudly when stepped on. Kyra knew where they were as well as how to avoid causing them to make any noise. She had discovered this while playing hide and seek with the twins. Many times Kyra had used this trick to sneak upstairs to hide while one of the twins would search the entire downstairs and backyard for her. She had them half-convinced that she knew how to teleport and could do it whenever she wanted. It kept them from messing with her too much when they were running around like little maniacs.

Now, however, this trick was being used in another manner. Her small tablet, which she had received on her birthday, was downstairs charging. She knew she wasn't supposed to go online without her parent's permission, but this sort of thing was something that she couldn't wait for. Plus, going downstairs, while not exactly against the rules, was something frowned upon by her parents. She needed to know how to build a Santa trap, and quickly. Sometimes an unspoken rule needed to be broken. Parents just didn't understand.

Kyra made her way past the squeaky steps and slid carefully across the hardwood floor to the kitchen, where all electronic devices were placed every night before bed. Very carefully she moved her device from the charger and went into the living room. It was very fortunate that Romeo was asleep up in the twin's room. The bulldog was usually all over her whenever the boys weren't around, and despite her parent's insistence that everything would be okay the bulldog had not been happy with the kaiju which had ended up in his old crate. The cranky dog had seemed put out by this intrusion and had ignored everything and everyone, except for his dinner of course. Kyra could not remember a time when the dog had missed a meal.

Besides, her plan would be much more difficult if Santa really did show up and Romeo started barking his head off at him. Then again, Romeo hadn't been bothered last year by Santa's arrival, so maybe there was a trick to his arrival which didn't set off dogs? It was something for her to ponder. She patiently waited for the device to power up before she opened a browser and began to search.

"Okay, let's see here," she whispered as she scrolled through the search results. She found one which looked easy and possible with household items, so she clicked on it. Immediately the instructions appeared on the screen. They were a little complicated with some words she didn't recognize so she skipped to the ingredients. She began to whisper them out loud. "Salt, five candles, some kind of rock in the center... wait a second. Oops. I meant 'How to Trap Santa', stupid machine. I hate autocorrect."

She tried a second time with the correct spelling and found a trick using only tinsel and a single bell. Which was helpful, because on the fireplace mantle was an old silver bell that had been Kyra's great-grandmother's many years before. In the storage closet near the front door was where they had put the Christmas decorations. Her mother had outlawed tinsel this year after the twins had managed to get it all over their bedroom the previous Christmas in what her father had called the "War on Cleanliness".

Kyra's check the clock on the mantle and saw that it was already eleven. She had no idea when Santa would be there, so she had to be ready. Moving quickly but quietly, Kyra managed to string the tinsel across the entrance of the fireplace before draping some along the floor. Next, she tied the silver bell onto some tinsel and strung it up across the floor between the sofa and the tree. Santa would trip on this and chime the silver bell, which - according to the helpful website she found - would stun him long enough for the tinsel to wrap itself around him. Kyra wasn't sure how the tinsel would do this, but she guessed that it was one of those things that would be obvious to her after it happened.

Once the tinsel was situated and the bell hung, it was time to wait. She yawned and checked the clock. Kyra was surprised to discover that it was almost midnight already. Time certainly had flown while she had prepared the Santa Trap. While she wasn't certain what time he would show up, Kyra was determined to make certain she was awake when he arrived.

Crawling into a dark corner behind her mother's creepy oversized nutcracker doll, Kyra settled down and began to wait. Time seemed to slowly drag as she yawned repeatedly, struggling to keep her eyes open as it crept ever so slowly to midnight. She sighed and leaned back into the corner.

"Just resting my eyes," she whispered drowsily as her eyes began to close. "A minute, maybe two."

Ding!

"Ugh," Kyra muttered as she shifted her back against the wall, half-asleep. "Mom, I don't wanna get up..."

Ding! Ding!

DING!

"Oh!" Kyra's eyes flew open. She

leapt to her feet and nearly screeched in alarm as she knocked over the nutcracker decoration. Managing to catch it before it fell to the ground and woke everyone else in the house up, she shifted it to rest against the edge of the sofa. She blinked and rubbed her eyes, then gasped loudly as the bell continued to make noise, albeit quietly now.

Kyra could not believe her eyes. She had to be dreaming. Giving herself a quick pinch, she continued to stare in disbelief. There, in the midst of tinsel and looking very confused, stood jolly old Saint Nick himself, Santa Claus.

CHAPTER 3 – THE REAL DEAL

“You’re real!” Kyra exclaimed breathlessly. Her plan had worked to perfection. She could feel her heart racing in her chest as she stared at Santa Claus. Her eyes narrowed suspiciously as she looked at the fireplace, then at the man in the red suit, then at the large red sack at his feet. “Wait… how did you fit down the chimney?”

“Magic,” Santa replied with a shrug. “Elf magic is top of the line in this business. You were always very smart, Kyra. Care to tell me why you have this elaborate but unnecessary trap set up?"

"This business?" she asked, her mind reeling as she struggled to catch up. Santa was definitely real. She needed to get a picture, so she picked up her tablet. A mangled cry escaped her lips. The battery was dead! She knew it had been charging for a few hours, so how could the battery be dead already? This was just a case of bad luck, she silently complained.

"Oh sure," Santa stated as he stroked his long white beard, seemingly oblivious to her problems with the tablet. "Modern chimneys are about as wide as a dinner plate now. My days of sliding down the chimney in this form are long past. Now? I just... well, you don't care really, do you? At the risk of repeating myself, why don't you tell me why you laid out such an elaborate trap to catch me in the act?"

"The baby kaiju!" Kyra exclaimed, remembering now why she had done this all in the first place. "My mom and dad thought there was a pug in the box, but it was a kaiju! How'd you switch it, and where did the pug go?"

"The pug is in a better place now," Santa said in a calm tone. He paused expectantly. Kyra's face scrunched up in horror and Santa, who must have realized what was going on in her mind, quickly explained. "Oh, no no no! Not like that! He's with a little boy up in Montreal. Nice family. Kid's probably going to be a veterinarian one day."

"But why'd you bring me a kaiju?" Kyra nearly wailed. Santa quickly tried to calm her down by handing her a candy cane.

"Here, eat this," he offered a red, green, and white sweet to her which he seemingly pulled out of the air. "It's a new type of candy cane, just invented by the elves. You know, you're an odd one."

"What do you mean?" Kyra asked as she tasted the candy cane. It was a strange mix of chocolate and jalapeno, which she loved separately but had never tried them together before. She found it oddly satisfying. It also, she noticed, distracted her from her earlier line of questioning.

"Most kids ask me the usual," Santa explained as he pulled out a few presents from his giant bag and began to place them under the tree. "What does Mrs. Claus look like? Are elves real? Do you really have eight tiny flying reindeer? Do you really live at the North Pole? That sort of stuff."

"Oh," Kyra said. "Uh... sorry?"

"No, it's quite all right," Santa waved away her concerns with a gloved hand. "It's rather refreshing and nice to be asked something different for a change."

"What do you mean? How often does this happen?" she asked, curious. Santa chuckled.

"I'll let you in on a little secret," he replied as he finished placing the presents beneath the tree. "I probably do this once or twice a year so the magic of Christmas remains strong. It might sound strange to you, but getting ‘caught’ is rather handy. You probably figured it out already, after all. You did use the tinsel. But where on Earth did you find a real silver bell?”

“It was my Nana Madeira’s,” Kyra answered softly. “She gave it to my mom.”

“Well, as often as I seem to get caught, nobody has ever used a real silver bell in ages.”

“That makes sense I guess,” Kyra said. She paused for a moment as she thought back to something Santa had said. “Wait. What did you mean by getting caught once or twice per year?”

“Magic,” Santa repeated as he made air quotes with his mittens. “Delivering the presents around the world doesn’t take up too much time. I spend most of the time drinking milk and eating cookies. Lately kids have been putting out gluten-free cookies. Let's just say that I am not a huge fan. But then again, cookies are cookies."

"Right," Kyra nodded, though she wasn't sure she completely understood. If it had been anyone else talking to her at that precise moment, she would have thought that perhaps they had drunk a little too much eggnog and fallen asleep on the couch like her Uncle Scott. She blinked and scowled at Santa, realizing that he had managed to distract her from the question. "Hey! You dodged my question!"

"Well, I just hadn't decided how to answer it yet," Santa reminded her. Kyra's eyes widened. Santa grabbed his bag and tossed it *up* the chimney. Somehow the oversized bag vanished up the narrow flute without any issue, leaving no evidence that it had been taking up a good portion of the living room floor in the first place. Santa turned and looked at her. "I don't have a good answer for you at this time. You need a while to think. I guess I better offer you the chance to save Christmas while we're waiting."

"Save... Christmas?" She asked, mystified. "Like they do in the movies?"

"Of course!" Santa's smile was wide. "You think people just come up with kooky ideas like that out of nowhere? Most of the movies came from stories of kids I had helped over the years. Discover the meaning of Christmas, saving the magic of Christmas, so on and so forth. I always have a blast doing these. Is it a cliché? Of course it is! But it's *fun!* And nobody can say Santa Claus does not know how to have a good time."

"I can't believe that Santa is asking me to help him save Christmas," Kyra muttered as she rubbed her eyes. "Am I dreaming?"

"Not that I'm aware," Santa said. "Though if you were, I'm sure I'd be the last person to tell you. However, I can assure you that you are not dreaming."

"Dreams are weird," Kyra stated, still slightly unconvinced. Her evening had gone from strange to downright bizarre in short order. "This sure feels real though."

"Dream or no dream, are you ready to save Christmas, Kyra?"

"Sure," she said. "What do we have to do?"

"First we have the grab little Georgie, and then we'll go and save Christmas," Santa said.

"Georgie?" Kyra frowned. "We need to take a boy?"

"Kinda," Santa waggled his mitten. "Georgie is what I call him. His full name is George Winston Salem Bigtooth."

"That's a weird name," Kyra said.

"Don't say that around him," Santa warned her. "He's a little sensitive about it."

"Well, 'Bigtooth' is a different last name."

"No, he's more embarrassed about being named George. It's why he goes by Georgie."

"Oh," Kyra yawned again and looked at the clock. Oddly enough, neither hand on the clock had moved past the twelve since she had first started talking to Santa. This shouldn't have been possible, but Kyra simply chalked it up to more of Santa's "elf magic". Or perhaps she really was dreaming? "Do I have time to grab my shoes before we go?"

"Well, of course," Santa said. "Time is relative. You know, it's–"

"Elf magic, yeah," Kyra said and turned to run back to the mud room.

"Oh, and don't forget to grab Georgie," Santa told her. Kyra paused and looked back at jolly old Saint Nick.

"Huh?"

"You know, Georgie," Santa's

smile remained wide, and there was a definitive twinkle in his eye. "The baby kaiju you have on the back porch."

"*That's* Georgie?"

"Of course it is," Santa replied. "Besides, we need Georgie to help us save Christmas!"

"How?"

"Well… I'm not really sure yet. But hey, there must be some reason why I stuck him in that box, right?"

"You don't even know why you stuck him in the box?" Kyra practically squealed.

"Child, I do a great many things in this world that even I don't understand," Santa beamed. "You think I remember switching out a single present on Christmas Eve? Ha! Mrs.

Claus had to remind me to harness all of the reindeer tonight because I tried to leave the North Pole with just Blitzen and Dasher. Forgot to drink my peppermint latte during the prep work. Can you believe it? Now, where were we?"

"Uh... saving Christmas?"

"Right!" Santa exclaimed, his laugh jolly. "Let's save Christmas!"

CHAPTER 4 – AND EIGHT... TINY REINDEER?

"C'mon Kyra, let's get moving," Santa said as Kyra struggled down the hallway carrying Georgie, who apparently was not pleased with being woken up and was squirming in her arms.

"Hold still," Kyra admonished the little kaiju as he squirmed. His big black eyes peered up at Kyra in confusion.

"Mrawp?"

"We're going to get you home," Kyra said as she shifted the kaiju into a more comfortable position. "But it would be a lot simpler if you would quit moving around so much."

"Mrawp!"

"Shush!" she hissed as the duo moved into the living room and to the front door. Very quietly, Kyra managed to get the door open and she took Georgie outside into the front lawn. Glad that Santa had suggested she get dressed for the journey before she picked up Georgie, she stepped out into the Christmas Eve with her pink fuzzy robe, sneakers, and pajama bottoms. Since she had stolen one of her father's t-shirts for sleepwear a long time ago and the habit had remained, her oversized top bore the words “Mr. Yuk Says No!” with a frowning face below it. Kyra didn’t get the reference but since the shirt was soft and warm, she had kept it even after her dad had complained.

She had pulled her long black hair into a ponytail so it would stay out of her face. Satisfied that she was ready to go, she looked around for Santa. However, there seemed to be no sign of him. Glancing upwards, she was surprised to see that he was not on her rooftop either.

“Where did he go?” she wondered aloud as she pulled Georgie tighter to her chest. It wasn’t too cold out but chilly enough for her to begin second guessing this decision. *Did Santa really think I can save Christmas*, she wondered.

She heard a noise around the

corner of the house and sighed. It would figure Santa would park his sleigh and the eight tiny reindeer by her father's shed. It was the best spot around to hide such a thing without nosy Mrs. McNealty getting involved. Moving quickly, she rounded the corner and came to a dead stop. Her eyes widened.

"Those are not eight tiny reindeer," Kyra muttered as she stared at the majestic creatures standing before her. Each one was bigger than a horse, and their antlers spread out wider than the sleigh.

"They're great, aren't they?" Santa asked as he tossed the massive bag into the back of the sleigh. "They can go from a standstill to Mach Four in less than two seconds. They're responsive to commands and can easily anticipate what I'm going to do next. Plus, they know the route and I get in one terrific nap while over the Pacific Ocean. Wonderful creatures."

"That's like stupid quick, isn't it?" Kyra asked as she wondered just how fast Mach Four was. It must have been very fast because she had heard about military jets only making it to Mach Two.

"Over three thousand miles per hour," Santa confirmed as he motioned at her. "The sleigh has a magic elf device to keep me from getting flattened and squished." He paused and shrugged after seeing the confused look on her face. "Physics. I break the laws of it, sure. But I still respect them, even if elf magic really makes fun of it on a routine basis. Relativity versus magic... well, there's a science paper I wouldn't want to be the author of!"

Kyra, who hadn't planned on having a physics discussion on her way to saving Christmas, changed the subject. "So where's Rudolph?"

Santa pointed up into the sky. Kyra followed his gesture and saw that there was not a cloud in sight. Santa explained. "I only let poor Rudolph join us on foggy or cloudy nights. Or if it's snowing really hard. He usually gets the European and Russian leg of the trip, and Donner rejoins us when I get to Australia. Though there was that one year in California that he had a blast with..."

"Is this thing safe?" Kyra asked as Georgie leapt from her arms and into the sleigh. The kaiju began to squawk loudly in excitement as he hopped around on the padded seat. He looked back at her expectantly. Kyra sighed. "Okay, fine. Give me a second."

"It's as safe as driving in a car," Santa chuckled. He easily slid into the front seat and grabbed the reins. "Safer, actually. We don't have to worry about other drivers. Just airplanes and the odd fighter jet who thinks we're violating restricted airspace. Seriously, almost collide with Air Force One a single time..."

"We won't be gone long, will we?" Kyra looked back at her house. "I don't want my parents to freak out if they check my room and see I'm gone."

"They won't even notice that you've left," Santa stated. "I promise."

"Well, okay," Kyra said and climbed into the sleigh. She looked around for a seat belt but couldn't find one. "Uh, Santa...?"

"No need," he told her. "I could fly this thing upside down and nothing would fall out."

"But how...? Right, magic," Kyra sighed.

"Now you're getting it," Santa's smile was contagious. "Magic!"

"I'm sneaking out at midnight with Santa Claus in order to save Christmas," Kyra muttered softly. "Of course it's magic."

"And we're off!" Santa exclaimed. "First stop to save Christmas? Hawaii!"

"Hawaii? Why Hawaii?" Kyra asked. Santa's smile was as wide as his face.

"Because we need to get directions!"

"Directions to where?"

"I don't know about you, young lady, but I've never been to the Isle of Monsters," Santa explained as the sleigh cruised through the air. "So we need to stop and ask for directions!"

"I thought you delivered presents everywhere?" Kyra asked. Santa clucked his tongue and shook his head.

"Hard to track a naughty or nice list on an island full of monsters," Santa explained. For a brief moment his smile almost seemed sad. "No matter how much I wish I could."

Kyra didn't really understand but she decided not to say anything. It was Santa's job, after all, to deliver presents to all the children in the world. He obviously knew what he was doing, even though Kyra didn't exactly agree with him about how he was doing it.

Conflicted, Kyra sat back in the seat, her arm draped around Georgie. She stared off, her mind lost in thought, as the sleigh rocketed through the night sky.

CHAPTER 5 – THE SHADOWS OF THE NIGHT

A light began to blink on Santa's dashboard, red and bright. A single bell chimed, and the sleigh suddenly dipped as Santa changed directions. Kyra looked over the edge of the sleigh and saw that the Rocky Mountains were below. She could see a few clusters of houses and guessed that they were probably over Utah. There was no way to be certain, though she could have sworn she caught a glimpse of a large lake far up to the north as they descended.

"Why are we stopping?" Kyra asked Santa as the wind began to whip around the sleigh. There was a decent-sized snow storm brewing up north, and it looked like it was headed towards them. "Are we in Utah?"

"Good guess," Santa replied as he steered the sleigh towards a snow-covered plain. There were no signs of houses in the immediate area, and the land was fairly flat. Kyra looked around and frowned. He hadn't answered the question so she repeated it.

"Why are we stopping here?"

"Quick meeting with an old friend," Santa explained as the sleigh made a perfect landing on the snowy ground. The reindeer kicked up a large cloud of the white powdery stuff as they came to a halt. The bells jingled pleasantly as the reindeer moved around a bit. "Well, I still consider him my friend, at least. Kyra, there's a bag in the back seat next to the gifts bag. It has carrots inside it. Would you be a dear and give one to each reindeer while we wait?"

"Uh, okay," she said before glancing down at the kaiju sleeping with his head pressed into her leg. So caught up in the sights and thrill of flying she had forgotten about Georgie. Apparently, the baby kaiju had decided that it was a perfect time to nap, and proceeded to do just that. She reached over and scratched behind his ear horn and he gave a very contented sigh. "Just like a dog," she murmured. Or a well-behaved cat, if there was such a thing.

Santa vaulted nimbly out of the sleigh and strode purposefully towards a small cluster of trees. Kyra began to pass out the carrots to each reindeer, all of whom seemed to gobble the vegetable with a single bite. They were enormous, taller than even her dad and all sprouted majestic antlers. On each harness was a name, and she began to hum under her breath as she moved down the line.

"Dasher, Dancer, Prancer, and Vixen," she ran a hand gently across the flank of the last reindeer, which turned his head slightly to look at her. She quickly jerked her hand away. "Sorry. I just... never mind. Great. Not only am I talking to a baby kaiju, now I'm apologizing to reindeer."

The massive reindeer remained placid, however, and turned its attention back towards the front. Feeling sheepish, Kyra looked around for any sign of Santa. She spotted him by the small copse of trees, apparently arguing with something in the shadows. Feeling nosy and having fed all the reindeer their carrots, she sidled over to where Santa Claus was.

"...and it's not too late for you," Santa was saying as she came within earshot. "The magic is still in you. You just need to believe."

"Believe?" a deep, mysterious voice seemed to mock Santa from the shadows. There was something sinister in the tone of voice. "How many times have you failed? Once? Twice? More than that? Please. Belief is something for kids. I'm not a kid anymore. My dreams have been crushed into dust because that's what happens, Santa, when reality hits you in the face."

"Your belief in the Christmas spirit is all that matters," Santa reminded him in a gentle voice. Kyra's ears perked up at this. What was going on?

"That's a load of bull and you know it," the sinister voice growled. "Have you told *her* yet? Does she know of her future, jolly old Saint Nick? The future of all children who believe in *you*?"

Santa turned to look at Kyra, his face sad as he realized Kyra had heard part of the argument. He sighed and shook his head. The shadow laughed.

"See? You can't even tell her the truth!" The voice mocked. "Christmas cheer is down, selfishness among the people is rising. People have forgotten about the spirit of it, only the gifts.

Greed rules. I can see it in her, even now. She was disappointed in the gift and not thankful for the spirit behind it. You think you can keep saving Christmas, year after year, with the help of a single child? You are more delusional than I thought, old man."

"I can help him!" Kyra suddenly protested. "I can help him save Christmas!"

"This year, perhaps," the voice allowed. A long, stick-like finger emerged from deep within the shadows and pointed directly at her chest. Kyra's heart practically leapt into her throat with fear. Whatever was in the shadows, it was terrifying. "The next? Or the one after? Greed clutches the hearts of humans, Claus. It only takes one child to allow greed to take hold for your fragile, protective hold over Christmas to shatter. Then the greed, want, and desires of the heart will overrule all, and there will be no more Christmas! No more gifting, but buying. No more family, just loneliness. The clock is ticking, old man. It's only a matter of time now. Time for all of us of the old to leave, forever. You can't fight fate."

"No!" Kyra shouted and clenched her fists defiantly. "Christmas will never die!"

"I will live long enough to see the end of you, Claus," the voice said as the bony finger retreated back into the darkness. "Better still, it will be I who ends it all. As you are so fond of saying, 'Ho... ho... ho'." The forbidding presence in the shadows suddenly ceased to be, leaving Kyra alone with Santa in the cold Utah mountains.

Santa sighed and rubbed the bridge of his nose with two fingers before turning back to look at Kyra.

"Who was that?" she asked.

"Someone I failed, a long time ago," Santa said in a tired voice. "Come now, we have to get to Hawaii. We still need to save Christmas."

"Is he going to be a problem?" Kyra asked as they trudged back to the sleigh. The good mood Santa had been in before the start of this crazy adventure had been dampened a bit. Now, Santa merely seemed tired. It made Kyra sad to watch. Kyra climbed into the sleigh and tapped Santa on the shoulder. "You didn't have to stop. You could have just, I don't know, avoided him."

"Can't avoid all your problems in

life, Kyra," Santa stated as the reindeer quickly gained altitude. They swung the sleigh to the left and suddenly were rocketing across the night sky once again. "Best if you deal with them in a manageable way, and quickly, or else they grow out of your control."

"But… he said he'd kill you!"

"No, he said he'd end me," Santa corrected gently. He gave her a sidelong look. "He's been trying to end the spirit of giving and charity for a very long time. He won't succeed this year, either. But I don't blame him. I don't get upset with him. It's just like the tale of the fox and the scorpion. He cannot change his way."

"Why would someone want to end Christmas?" Kyra asked. She had never heard of a tale about foxes and scorpions, though she had seen a movie about a fox and a hound once. It had made her cry. Which wasn't a bad thing, except it had been at school and a few of the boys made fun of her.

"Why do people think it's okay to ruin the hopes and dreams of others?" Santa asked and shook his head. His normally kind eyes were filled with sadness as he continued to speak, his voice soft and sad. "Humans... are a beautiful and terrible creature, capable of limitless compassion and unfathomable cruelty."

"He... he's *human*?"

"He was, a long time ago," Santa confirmed. An all-too familiar twinkle reappeared in the corner of his eye. "Let's not worry about him. Onwards to Hawaii, and then the Isle of Monsters."

"To save Christmas," Kyra

murmured. In her heart she was still excited about the idea of saving Christmas, but after seeing the creature in the shadows and how twisted his words were, she began to wonder if saving Christmas was all she should be doing. *Maybe there's something more I can do to help?*

CHAPTER 6 – MELE KALIKIMAKA

The journey over the Pacific Ocean took very little time it seemed. One moment they had been flying over the fog-covered San Francisco Bay Bridge, the next they were approaching the Hawaiian Islands. It was amazing to behold. It was almost as if Santa had decided that Kyra needed to see the bright lights of the big city before whisking them through the boring flight over thousands of miles of water until he had announced that they were finally over the Hawaiian Islands.

"Beautiful, isn't it?"

Attention drawn by Santa's question, Kyra peered down through the thin cloud cover at the sights below. The peak of Mauna Loa was surrounded by fog, and just below it she could see another volcano as lava flowed brightly in the darkness. It was both terrifying and magical, a sight that she thought that she would never see. It was also the first volcanic eruption that she had ever laid eyes on, and desperately hoped to be the last.

"Hina is a moon goddess of the Hawaiian peoples," Santa explained as the sleight began to descend surprisingly close to one of the lava fields on the south end of the island. "She's a very sweet lady who is quiet and reserved usually. Since she sees everything in the Pacific Ocean at nighttime when the moon is out, she'll know exactly where the Isle of Monsters is. Assuming she will help us."

"Uh huh," Kyra said as they settled down onto a strip of road which hadn't yet been devoured by the approaching lava. She eyed it as Santa hopped out of the sleigh and began to search his pockets. He grunted and twisted his body for a moment before he fished out a large item from his back pocket. Kyra's eyes widened as she recognized it. "That's a conch! Where... how'd that fit in your pocket?"

"Elf magic," Santa proclaimed as he lifted the tan-colored shell to his mouth. He whispered a few words into it, most of which were muted for Kyra. She did catch one which stood out, however. It just didn't make any sense to her.

"What does *kirihemete* mean?" asked Kyra as she got out of the sleigh. Santa winked at her.

"Secret word so she knows who's trying to get in contact with her," Santa explained. "I just told her it was Father Christmas calling. Now, we wait and see if she's listening."

"Will it take long?" Kyra asked as she looked back at the lava which was flowing slowly but steadily down the slopes of the volcano in the distance. She glanced back at Santa, who did not appear to be at all concerned with the impending doom. While it wasn't exactly hot, it was warm enough for her to wish she had shorts on.

"Not long at all, dear child," a

sweet, musical voice said from directly behind Kyra. She turned around and yelped as a woman had mysteriously appeared. Kyra gawked. Dressed in a comfortable looking purple robe of some sort and a lei around her neck, she was the perfect image of precisely what a goddess of the moon should look like to Kyra. Hina's black hair was long, much like Kyra's, but with curls, a stark contrast to Kyra's straight locks. The moon goddess' face was round and beautiful, her eyes a brown that Kyra only wished she could have. "*Aloha* Kyra, Santa."

"Hello," Kyra said shyly. She tucked her chin down and tried to be inconspicuous. The moon goddess was majestic in form and had a calming presence about her. Kyra suddenly wished she were as pretty as the goddess, though she could not explain why.

"Where did you get the baby kaiju from?" Hina asked in surprise as Georgie, having woken from his nap, had stuck his tiny head over the edge of the sleigh to see just what was going on. He spotted the moon goddess and seemed to bark at her. A solid *thump! thump! thump!* could be heard by all as the kaiju's tail slammed against the inside of the sleigh in excitement. Hina laughed and clapped her hands together, delighted. "He is adorable! I thought this species of kaiju died out ages ago! Wherever did you find him?"

"That's Georgie," Kyra told Hina, somehow finding the courage to speak. "I think Santa swapped him out in one of my presents. We're taking him back to the Isle of Monsters so he can be with his own kind."

"Why?" Hina asked as she looked at Kyra. There was a strange expression upon her face. "The baby kaiju – Georgie? – has already become *ohana* to you. He knows no one else and will accept no other. Why do you wish for this to change?"

"I know that word," Kyra said as she scrunched up her nose. "Ohana means family, right?"

"Yes, family," Hina nodded. "He has accepted you as his. I cannot think of the right word for what has happened. Santa*, a hoopaa?* Kyra, why do you wish to leave him?"

"Ah, I believe that word you're looking for is 'bonded', Hina," Santa clarified.

"He can't stay with me!" Kyra protested. "My family… neighbors are weird. He's just..."

"Different," Hina murmured in a quiet voice. "I understand your confusion and fear, *keiki.*"

"It's Kyra," she corrected the goddess as sad memories of her grandmother came to mind. Nana Madeira had been the only woman to call Kyra "Kiki", and her death still hurt, two years later. Hina cocked her head and smiled softly.

"*Keiki* is Hawaiian for 'child', Kyra," the moon goddess explained. "I'm sorry if I hurt you. Some injuries still cause pain long after they become nothing but old scars. Please, forgive me."

"It's okay," Kyra said, slightly embarrassed. She had not meant to snap at Hina. "I shouldn't have..." her voice trailed off. Hina approached Kyra and, surprising the young girl, gave her a big hug.

"Never be ashamed of your emotions," Hina told her. "They are who you are."

"I appreciate you coming, Hina," Santa said, interrupting the two. "I am in need of your help."

"And I am in need of yours," Hina stated. "How can I be of service, Nicholas?"

"You need our help?" Kyra asked as she looked up at the goddess. "Really?"

"Indeed."

"We need directions to take Georgie here to his home," Santa explained, obviously missing Hina's request for help. "I know that the island is around here somewhere, but..."

"You need to know precisely where," the moon goddess nodded. "Are your reindeer as fast as I remember?"

"Of course," Santa grinned.

"Then simply fly over the Big Island and head directly north," Hina told them. "After flying for about one hour at their top speed you should arrive at *Mokupuni*. You won't be able to miss it. It has a volcano much like this that is very active. You should see it from miles away."

"I thank you for your assistance, Hina," Santa said. He motioned to Kyra. "Time to fly, little girl."

"Wait," Kyra held up a hand. She looked at Hina curiously. The Moon Goddess had helped them. It was only right to try and return the favor. "You said you needed our help?"

"We're on a tight schedule Kyra, remember?" Santa reminded her. His tone was stern, but there was definitely a twinkle in his eye.

"She helped us," Kyra stated in a firm voice. "We should help her."

"Mrawrp!" Georgie agreed from the sleigh.

"Well, that sounds settled then," Santa said with a huge smile and a loud belly laugh. "How may we be of service to you, Hina?"

"My earring," she said as she reached up to touch her naked ear with a fingertip. "The *nuanai* fishmen stole it eons ago, and I have been confined to the mortal plane ever since. I hate to ask, since they are very dangerous, but with your friend there accompanying you, it should be a relatively easy task for you to complete."

"Kyra does seem to be pretty competent," Santa nodded as he stroked his thick white beard. "I would be glad to help."

"Me too!" Kyra exclaimed.

"Mrawp!" Georgie added, his eyes wide in excitement. Kyra smiled and laughed at the baby kaiju's enthusiasm.

Hina spotted this as well and grinned. "The kaiju has a pure heart, and he is easy to understand. I thank all of you for your help."

"Are those fishmen still down by Howland Island?" Santa asked. Hina nodded.

"Yes," she answered. "It shames me to admit that they mock me by parading my pearl earring around in the light of the moon. I have no power there, since they are protected by a circle of *ahi*. Please, if you do this, be careful."

"I've survived much worse over the years," Santa said as he slid into the front seat of the sleigh. "I'll be fine."

"It's not you who I am warning, Nicholas," Hina corrected him as her gaze drifted down to Kyra, who shifted uncomfortable. "Santa is pretty much immortal, *keiki*, but you are not. Please, use caution when dealing with the *nuanai*. They are very dangerous."

"Uh, okay," Kyra said as Hina engulfed her in another warm hug. Kyra sighed as the sounds and smells of the sea overwhelmed her. For just a moment it felt as though her Nana Madeira was there with her. An unwelcome tide of emotions welled to the surface and Kyra began to cry. She sniffled and coughed as she realized that she had left tears on Hina's robe. "I'm sorry."

"There is nothing to be sorry for," Hina told her in a gentle tone. "The love you have for your grandmother? Never apologize for this."

"Thank you, Hina," Kyra said. "I guess we'll see you after we get the earring back."

"No," Hina told her. "Once the earring is out of the clutches of the *nuanai*, I will be able to reclaim it.

Simply exit the circle of *ahi* with the earring, expose it to the moonlight, and all will be well."

"Okay," Kyra said and stepped away from the moon goddess. "It was nice to meet you."

"The pleasure is all mine, Kyra," Hina replied. "You are a special little girl. Do not rush in your decisions, for you will come to the right one eventually."

"I won't," Kyra promised and ran to the sleigh. She turned to wave at Hina but saw that she had already left. Kyra lowered her hand and slipped into the sleigh next to Georgie, who immediately crawled onto her lap. His big black eyes looked into hers and she absentmindedly began to scratch his left horn.

"Mrawrp?" Georgie chirped at her. Kyra shrugged.

"I don't know, buddy," she said, her mind lost in thought and completely unaware that she was having a conversation with a baby kaiju. "I don't know if we'll ever see her again."

"Mrawp..." Georgie sighed and nestled into her arms. She held him tightly as Santa's reindeer began to pull the sleigh high in the sky. After a final turn above Manoa Loa they angled south and headed towards the water home of the *nuanai*, or fishmen as Santa had called them. Kyra closed her eyes as an emotional wave of confusion and shame washed over her.

On one hand, she knew that sending Georgie to live with his own kind was what anyone else would do.

All animals belonged in the wild with members of their species. It was just the right thing to do. But then, Georgie wasn't exactly a stray bird or anything remotely close. He was a kaiju. Kyra couldn't be certain, but she could not help but to wonder whether or not normal rules applied to a creature who might one day destroy Tokyo.

On the other hand... well, there really wasn't any other hand in the equation. She simply could not have Georgie in the house. Her parents would freak out if she brought him back, the neighbors would complain and call animal control or the army if they saw him in the back yard, and there was always the possibility that the silly little kaiju might get hungry and eat Romeo the dog one day. Her brothers would *not* be happy if that occurred.

No, Kyra decided. She was doing the right thing. She just wished that she felt better about it.

CHAPTER 7 – THE FIRE RING

“So I guess I can assume that *ahi* means ‘fire’, right?” Kyra asked as she leaned over the edge of the sleigh. Half-turning, she shot Santa a look. “Why am I not surprised you never said anything before.”

“Well, I didn’t want to discourage you,” Santa said as he deftly steered the sleight into a wide circular orbit around the smoking volcano. While the lava flow was as bright and easily seen as Hani had promised, the moon goddess had neglected to mention that a lagoon surrounded it, and beyond that was a near-perfect circle of islands, all of which seemed to be on fire. If there had been any plant life on any of the islands, they had since long burned up due to the immense heat. In fact, as far as Kyra could tell, there was nothing on any of the islands which would allow the fires to burn.

Yet there they were, flames leaping off the sand, lighting the islands for miles around. Kyra sighed and sat back down in the sleigh. It should have been physically impossible. Then again, she was in a sleigh high in the air with Santa Claus, a baby kaiju sitting on her lap, eight reindeer the size of Clydesdales pulling the sleigh, and on a mission hunting for a magic pearl earring of a Hawaiian moon goddess. Kyra's life had become surprisingly complicated in a hurry. All she had wanted to do was to get a puppy.

"I have a rough idea of a plan, but I'm open to suggestions," Santa told her as the sleigh began to slow down. He pointed one gloved hand towards an island which didn't seem to be burning as much as the others. "I bet that's the way into the area where the *nuanai* live. I mean, they're fishmen, right? They probably aren't big fans of fire."

"Mrawp!" Georgie agreed.

"Okay, that sounds fine and all, but what *are* they?" Kyra asked, curious. "Are they men with gills? Fish with legs? Half man, half fish? Are they like shark men? Or dolphins? Wait, no. Dolphins are mammals, not fish. What about swordfish?"

"I really don't know," Santa admitted. He then laughed heartily. "Ho ho ho! This is turning out to be quite an adventure, wouldn't you agree?"

"Yeah, I guess," Kyra muttered as she stared out at the burning islands. "Kidnap Santa, go on an adventure, get terrified by a dark and mysterious being in a forest, meet a moon goddess, take a baby kaiju to an island filled with monsters, and save Christmas. In the movies kids simply fly around showing the true meaning of Christmas to their parents, who have forgotten. I've never seen a Christmas movie with Santa taking a child on this sort of adventure."

"That's because television executives have no sense of flair or style," Santa said, his tone jovial.

It seemed to Kyra almost nothing could dampen his spirits. "It's rather sad. They always portray a big city, Santa crashing into some building or another... I'm a much better pilot than that. Plus, the reindeer aren't dumb. They avoid everything that can hurt the sleigh. Besides, our adventure is much grander in scale! Who wouldn't want to see Santa, a young girl, and her pet baby kaiju save Christmas? The ratings alone would mean for multiple sequels! Imagine it! 'Kyra and Santa Save Earth From Martians'."

"Martians are real?" she asked him. Santa shrugged.

"I don't know," he admitted. "Never met one. But it would be a great television show!"

Kyra couldn't argue with that. She knew that she would watch that show in a minute, as would her brothers. Probably all of her friends, too. Maybe even her parents as well.

"We definitely need a plan," Kyra said as she watched the flames dance along the shores of the beach. Her brow furrowed as she concentrated. "Santa, do you know how the sand burns like that?"

"Magic?" Santa shrugged. He gave her an apologetic look. "Sorry. It's my go-to answer for everything I don't understand. That, or it's quantum mechanics. Which I also don't understand."

"Magic works," Kyra admitted. She recalled a line from a movie her family had gone to see the year before, where the hero told his friends that if you go far enough back in time, any technology could seem like magic. The tablet she had left behind at her house probably would have gotten her burned at the stake for witchcraft in the 1600s, for example. Besides, quantum mechanics was not something she knew about. "Hey, look. The flames are dying down."

"So they are," Santa said. "Strange. Do you have a plan in mind?"

"Can't we fly above the flames and then, I don't know, land on the water?" Kyra suggested. "They're magic reindeer. Can they float? Can the sleigh float?"

"Yes, the sleigh can float," Santa agreed. "The reindeer can swim."

"But they can fly," Kyra countered as a plan began to form. "Does your sleigh have an autopilot or anything?"

"Kyra, that's brilliant!" Santa said as he half-turned in his seat. He reached into his large Christmas bag and rummaged around on the inside for a few seconds before he found what he was looking for. With a cry of triumph, he pulled out a pair of flippers and a matching pair of goggles. "We set the autopilot on and let the reindeer orbit from above after they drop us off. You use the flippers and dive down to fetch the pearls from the *nuanai*, and we make our escape."

"The only problem with that plan is that I don't know how to scuba," Kyra pointed out. "I also don't swim very well. Oh, and I don't breathe underwater. Boring, uninteresting girl here with no magical talents whatsoever. Well, not true. You can ask my brothers. I fall down *very* well."

"Hold on, I have something that can help with the underwater thing," Santa said as he shoved the goggles and fins back into his bag. He reached into his large coat pocket and withdrew an item. He held it out for Kyra to see. "Forgot I had this."

"A knife?" Kyra asked, confused.

"Ah, but not just any old knife," Santa answered as he turned the sheathed blade over in his hands. The scabbard which contained the blade was silver with two green gemstones embedded within. A small leather strap was attached to it. "This was wielded by the Japanese sea god Watatsumi, a gift from the great Izanagi. Or he stole it from Izanagi in the dead of night. Who really knows? The history of that knife - it's called a *tanto* by the way - is a little sketchy. I don't know if it's really from Japanese mythology or not, but I do know that it allows the wielder to breathe underwater and walk amongst the sea as though the bearer were on dry land. At least, that's what the kappa told me when they gave it to me."

"Uh..." Kyra's night just continued to get weirder by the minute. She understood about one in three things Santa just told her. "What's a kappa?"

"Magic creature. Doesn't matter right now," Santa said as he carefully handed her the dagger-sized blade. "I'll explain them later. Maybe, if I don't forget. I do that sometimes. What was I... oh, right. Be careful if you draw the blade from the scabbard. It's really sharp."

"Still not clear about how I'm supposed to deal with the *nuanai* if they try to stop me," Kyra said, unconvinced.

"We can take Georgie, too," Santa said. Poking Georgie's rotund tummy, he laughed. "You'll scare those big bad fishmen, won't you?"

"Mrawp!"

"I don't know..." Kyra's voice trailed off. Shaking her head, she sighed. It was crazy, but crazy enough that it just might work. She'd captured Santa, flew across the country, and met a moon goddess in Hawaii. This? This should be easy. "You know what? Let's do this."

"Kyra, we should probably have a plan–"

"We walk in like we own the place, grab the earring, and get out as fast as possible," Kyra stated, interrupting Santa. "Most of beating an opponent is attitude, the rest is practice. That's what my hockey coach says. When he's not yelling at us for pretending to not know how to skate, I mean."

"Okay then" old Saint Nick said. The sleigh shifted and they began to descend inside the ring of fire. They drew close to the beach where they had noticed the flames weren't as strong. It was surprisingly cool there. Santa reached over and pressed a button on the console of his sleigh. He then looked at the reindeer. "Okay boys, come down in half an hour, then every five minutes after. If I'm not back in an hour, go get help."

"From Mrs. Claus?" Kyra asked, curious.

"Nope," came the reply. "The Etru."

"Etru?"

"The Elf Tactical Retrieval Unit," Santa explained. "I just call it E.T.R.U. for short."

"Now you're just making things up," Kyra muttered under her breath as she slipped the sheathed dagger into the pocket of her robe. She scooped up Georgie and leapt onto the beach.

"I don't think that even I can invent something that silly," Santa joked. "If I were making it up, I would have called it TREATS - Tactical Retrieval Elf Application Technology, Secret. The jokes would have written themselves. Besides, I'm really hard to capture."

"I caught you with tinsel and a silver bell," she reminded him. "And TREATS? Really?"

"You got lucky with that silver bell. But seriously, I'm not one with many original ideas, after all. That's what I have the elves for."

Georgie scrambled out of her arms and landed on the sandy beach. He looked around for a moment, sniffing the air, before he let out a satisfied grunt. Moving quickly, the little kaiju began to move towards the water on the inside of the ring of flaming islands. The lagoon was a deep blue in color, darker than the waters on the outside. Kyra had seen enough nature shows on television to know that this meant the water was deep here, deeper than it should have been due to the erupting volcano and islands around it. It should have been shallow and a light blue in color, and easy to see the ocean floor beneath it.

Kyra swallowed nervously, her fingers reaching into her pocket to touch the dagger Santa had given her. Ahead of her, Georgie made another odd noise and began to shake his body like a wet dog. His scales rippled in the light of the volcano as the movement continued. Suddenly, a large fin popped out of the kaiju's back. Four more similar but slightly smaller followed suit until Georgie had a ridge of fins protruding out of his back.

"Mraaaaawp!" Georgie cried out in triumph, his claws reaching for the sky. Kyra couldn't help but giggle a little at the sight of her baby kaiju acting big and tough, even though he was no larger than a basketball.

"You've got my back, don't you?" she asked the red baby kaiju in a soft tone. Georgie looked over his should at her and he seemed to smile. It was weird. Sometimes she could almost swear that the little kaiju could understand what she was saying. Of course, Kyra oftentimes felt as though she knew exactly what Georgie was trying to say back to her.

"Okay, I think we're ready to go in," Santa said as he joined her on the shores of the small island. He looked around for a moment and whistled. "I wonder how it stays on fire all the time? It's not that hot here, all things considered."

"Magic?" Kyra suggested with a shrug. "Seems to be the answer for just about anything."

"This is why I always get scolded by kids who want a science kit for Christmas," Santa groused as he looked up as his sleigh shot off into the sky. He frowned. "I sure hope they understood the instructions. If not, it's a long swim back to land. Oh well. Onwards, and to adventure!"

Kyra took a deep breath and pulled the dagger out of its sheath from the pocket of her fuzzy robe. With a nervous glance back at Santa, she began to step towards Georgie and the water. Her heart was racing in her chest and she felt as if it were about to explode from nervousness. It hadn't even been this bad when they had first taken off in Santa's sleigh back at her house.

She felt no water as she stepped into the sea, however. It was if a barrier was pushing the water away from her foot. Her shoes remained dry, as did her fuzzy pink robe. Amazed, Kyra stepped further into the water. It felt as though she were walking on dry land. She was not floating like when she went swimming at the community pool. The magic dagger seemed to be working as Santa had said it would.

"C'mon Georgie," she said and continued forward. "Let's go find these *nuanai* and get Hina's pearl earring back."

"Mrawp!"

"Wait for me, Kyra," Santa said as he moved into the water next to her. His suit seemed to be soaking up every single drop of water in the ocean. His bright red coat was quickly turning a deep maroon color as water continued to become lodged in it. His black boot began to make a horrid squelching sound with every step he took. Santa frowned and stroked his beard as a starfish, which had apparently been wandering in the surf, attached itself to Santa's knee. "Well, this is peculiar. My magic isn't letting me phase through the water. I'm a horrible swimmer. This could end badly for me."

"You're not coming with?" Kyra asked, frightened.

"It doesn't appear that I can," Santa admitted after a moment. He lifted his boot out of the water and pulled it off. Turning it sideways, he dumped out the water – as well as a small crab which had somehow managed to crawl inside. He shook his head and frowned. "No, I think I'm stuck on land for this one, Kyra."

"I... I think we can handle this, Santa," Kyra said, though there was a bit of hesitation in her voice. Could she, though? There was some uncertainty in her heart. She carefully unsheathed the small sword Santa had gifted her and handed him the scabbard. He carefully took it, nodding in approval. Santa looked at her for a moment before he winked.

"I believe you can," he agreed. "The two of you are a very formidable team, Kyra. Take care of Georgie and he will take care of you. Remember, the *nuanai* are dangerous. Be very careful."

"I will," Kyra promised. She took another deep breath and exhaled. Closing her eyes, she stepped fully into the water. The faint sensation of the ocean rushing over her head could not be ignored, and her eyes opened. They went wide as she saw *everything*.

Instead of a deep blue clouding her vision, she could see far and wide.

A large pyramid structure lay off in the distance, near where she estimated the center of the deep lagoon was. More small buildings, very similar in design to adobe houses she had seen once while researching the Hopi Indians of the southwest. Except, as far as Kyra could tell, these houses were made completely out of coral and seashells.

Georgie swam past her, his powerful and thick tail propelling him quickly along. His direction changed suddenly and Kyra watched as he snatched a large fish which happened to swim a tad too closely to the kaiju. Georgie swallowed the large fish in two gulps. Kyra tensed up slightly as she realized that the little kaiju could eat something almost twice his size, and that there was now blood in the water.

She'd seen how it works on TV.

Blood in the water eventually meant sharks would show up. Sharks that would undoubtedly be larger than she was, which meant they would be easily big enough to eat Georgie in one, maybe two bites. Unsure if there were any in the immediate area and not wanting to wait around to see, Kyra began to hurry.

The closer she came to the underwater village of the *nuanai*, the more anxious she became. The fishmen had to be somewhere around, yet the only thing that Kyra could see was empty paths between their homes. The houses glinted brightly in the lava light, which seemed to cause everything to glow around her. It was ethereal and stunning, a beauty that rivaled everything else. The rainbow-colored shells seemed to change color as she passed by, changing through every variety of color as the light dance across them.

Looking around, Kyra saw the true purpose of the shells. The reflecting light attracted small tuna, which in turn seemed to draw larger fish to come and eat them. These, in turn, were then caught by the *nuanai*. Kyra spotted more than a few nets for catching fish positioned between some of the houses.

"Fishmen eating fish?" Kyra wondered aloud for a moment. "Is that like a pig eating bacon? Ugh, gross. I don't want that idea in my head."

"Mrawp!" Georgie exclaimed as he swam by, chasing the smaller fish. It didn't appear as though he were hunting them. In fact, it appeared to Kyra that he was acting more like a sheepdog and herding the fish around.

A fun game for the kaiju from the looks of it, she thought.

"Don't wander too far, Georgie," Kyra admonished him as she continued to look around. Though she wasn't entirely certain how the tiny little monster could protect her, his presence did make her feel better about exploring the underwater area without Santa's help.

"Mrawp!" came a quick reply and Georgie obediently swam closer to her. Reaching out with his claws, he grabbed hold of her robe at her shoulder and attached himself to her. Oddly enough, though Georgie was wet from his swimming, the dagger seemed to be keeping him out of the water now as well. It was all very strange.

"I guess this thing works on

anything touching me. Cool."

Out of the corner of her eye she saw something large move. Whirling, she caught a glimpse of something dark and green sliding behind one of the homes of the *nuanai*. Georgie began to growl in a deep tone, warning whatever that remained out of sight to not come closer. Kyra brandished the small sword before her like a talisman, waving it back and forth as she kept an eye out for something big and green.

"Georgie, I think we're being watched," Kyra hissed as more movement could be seen on the edge of her vision. Every time she turned to get a better look, however, it had vanished. Ahead of them the temple loomed. Kyra felt a slight tickle in her throat and coughed nervously. "I bet the earring is in that large, seashell covered building over there. It looks like the type of place to be all big and scary on the outside, and then looks nice inside."

"Mrawwrraaaaap," Georgie warned, his normal tone shifting to a low and guttural sound. He too seemed to be growing more nervous by the second as their unseen adversaries stalked them. Hissing, a long tongue flicked out and tasted the air, like a snake would. His eyes were tracking all the movement around them. "*Mrawwwwp.*"

"I know, buddy," she whispered. The *nuanai* were staying just on the peripheral edge of her vision, out of sight but letting her see faint glimpses of them as they followed the duo towards the mysterious-looking temple in the center of the village. "I take it back. It's probably scary on the inside, too."

"Mrawp," Georgie agreed.

Kyra swallowed nervously. Her hands were beginning to sweat as they clutched the small sword tightly. She stopped at the seashell stairs leading up to the temple and looked back. Shadows lingered at the edge of the village but she still could not see their true forms. Much like the entity Santa had met with in the Utah wilderness, the beings which sought to stop them from rescuing Hina's pearl earring preferred the shadows to remain behind, hiding their true forms from the light. She did not understand why, though there was something to be said about being tormented by the unseen.

"They're shadows because the light doesn't reach," Kyra whispered something her mother had told her once, late in the night after a nightmare had woken her up from a solid sleep. Kyra's mother had held her and comforted her while the last terrors of the nightmare fled. "Show them the light and the shadows will flee."

She was so far out of her depth here. Which was funny, given the fact she was currently walking along the bottom of the ocean floor without a single drop of water on her. Her father would have appreciated the joke. He was a natural punster who would driver her and her mother nuts during long drives, trying to outdo the twins with horrible puns. Plus, dad jokes were his thing.

"Mrawp?" Georgie asked her. Swallowing, she nodded.

"Yeah buddy. I think we need to

go inside."

"Mrawp," Georgie did not sound pleased but then, neither was Kyra. The absolute last thing she wanted to do was to enter a temple which could be filled with fishmen.

Kyra squared her shoulders and took a deep, calming breath. A promise was a promise, and Kyra had assured Hina she would do all she could to help retrieve her earring. Even if it meant going through the dark and scary-looking entrance.

"Georgie? Time to go inside and find the earring," she told the baby kaiju. Steeling herself, she walked through the dark alcove and into the temple, Georgie right behind her. "Wow," Kyra said and looked around. "It's much bigger on the outside."

Indeed it was. She had expected a large and ornate interior with lots of shells and whatever else the *nuanai* used for their decorations. The plain, small room inside felt more like a chapel than some grand cathedral. However, the item she was searching for was in clear view. The pearl was set in the middle of a clamshell, beneath a small mirror which seemed to reflect the moonlight onto it. Kyra understood now just why Hina was so upset with the fishmen. They were taunting her by allowing her to catch a glimpse of the pearl but not allowed to get her earring back.

"That's just mean," Kyra grumbled. One thing she hated more than her brothers going into her room without permission was bullies. Bullies were the kind of people she tried to avoid because it was almost never worth the trouble. Unless they were picking on someone. If she saw something, she always spoke up and tried to put a stop to it.

"That is one big horking earring," Kyra observed as she approached the small altar. The softball-sized pearl shimmered in the light as it sat atop a pile of crushed white seashells, which in turn were surrounded by a bed of small black pebbles. It was a gorgeous setup, and Kyra wondered for a moment how cool it would look in an aquarium back home. She paused and reconsidered the size of the pearl. "Well, she *is* a moon goddess. It probably fits her real form well enough."

"Mrawp," Georgie warned from a little distance away. Kyra looked back over her shoulder and saw the baby kaiju swimming around at the entrance, protecting it. Even though the *nuanai* were larger than Georgie, they were definitely afraid of him. They were gurgling in their strange language, obviously agitated that Kyra was taking back what they had stolen.

"Keep them away, Georgie," Kyra said as she grabbed the pearl with her free hand. There was barely enough room in her robe pocket for it, but she managed to shove it down without too much issue. With a sigh, she turned to leave. "Okay Georgie, let's get out of here."

Still brandishing the dagger before her, she quickly made her way out of the small chamber and back into the village proper. The *nuanai* had gathered around, all armed with some type of rudimentary weapon. She gasped as she got her first full look at them

They were a shiny blue color, matching the seashells which decorated their homes. Their faces looked more like fish than people, though they did have shoulders like humans. Instead of hair they had more fish scales and their hands were shaped into claws. Each one of them looked angry at her. She understood their anger, even if it was misplaced. She was merely returning an object to the rightful owner.

None, however, dared to come too close. Their fear of Georgie outweighed their desire to keep the stolen pearl earring.

As Kyra and Georgie moved through the village, the fishmen became more and more agitated. It was obvious to her that they were irritated. Georgie, who had swum closer to her, watched the *nuanai* closely, his head jerking side to side. He hissed as one dared to get closer. The fishman pulled back, wary. She had no idea why Georgie scared them so, but she intended to take full advantage of it.

"Stay close to me," she told the tiny kaiju.

"*Mrawrp*," Georgie agreed and brushed ever so lightly against her arm. His warm scales were comforting as the *nuanai* watched them in stony silence. What would have been just a tad creepy was made much more terrifying by the absolute lack of sound made by the alien-like fishmen.

The dim light from the ring of fire nearby caused a shimmering effect throughout the water, every color of a rainbow dancing across the sandy ocean floor. They were getting close to the shore but it was still deep enough for Kyra to hang on to the *tanto.* She didn't understand it but felt as though soon she would be forced to get rid of the small sword.

The *nuanai* suddenly swarmed towards her *en masse*. Terrified, she swung the small sword at them. They broke away in two different directions, swimming around her similar to the way sharks circle prey. She turned and dodged as one of the fishmen tried to grab her robe. She smacked him with the flat of the blade and he swam away. Georgie made a funny noise from not to far away. More fishmen were around her and she lost track completely of where she was.

Kyra began to run but the magic of the sword felt weaker. The cold of the ocean pressed in against her and the currents began to push sideways. The edges of the robe began to get wet as the magical field around her failed. Instinct told her to take a deep breath and hold on because things were about to get weird.

Kyra was suddenly soaked as the water around her finally broke through the magical barrier the small sword had created around her. She almost gasped from the surprising shock of cold water as it hit her. Fortunately, she remember where she was and managed, just barely, to hang on to her air even as the pressure of all the water bore down on her. She began to swim, tossing the small sword aside. The *nuanai* began to follow but quickly lost interest as they spotted the magical sword. The fishmen swarmed around it and they quickly disappeared into the dark waters.

Georgie! Kyra silently screamed. There was no more light, only darkness, and her lungs were burning from a lack of oxygen. She kept paddling what felt like up, chest bursting as she fought to reach the surface. *Don't panic. Don't panic.*

It had been her father's favorite mantra, one he repeated over and over again. If she or her brothers were ever in trouble, the worst possible thing they could do was to panic. It was okay to be scared. In fact, it was almost expected to be afraid at some point. But, he always said, it was how one dealt with the fear which decided what would happen next.

Steady, she silently told herself.

Remain calm. You got this, girl. There's no reason to panic. It's just water. You swim all the time. You can do this.

Kyra looked up. The surface was nowhere in sight. She wasn't going to make it.

Suddenly something grabbed her arm and tugged upwards. She almost screamed, which would have ended things quite abruptly. Her heart felt like it was going to explode out of her chest until she recognized the shape of her baby kaiju.

Georgie had come back for her! She could have kissed his pointed little snout. With his tiny little claw he gripped her bathrobe arm and, with a powerful swish of his tail they were suddenly accelerating towards the surface. Her vision began to gray and her head felt funny. Sleep beckoned and she wanted to nap so much it hurt. Could she stay awake long enough?

Cold air suddenly slapped her in the face and she gasped, inhaling a massive breath of sweet, sweet air. The gray which had been surrounding her eyesight was gone. Oddly enough, the ring of fire was gone as well. She tread water for a moment before she found Santa, though there was no sign of the reindeer or sleigh. He wasn't too far away from her. It shocked her to see she was so close to the tiny little island they had landed upon hours earlier.

Georgie's tiny horned head popped up out of the water next to her. If kaiju could grin then she was almost certain the baby was smiling from horn to horn. He seemed immensely pleased with himself. Kyra laughed a little as she began to doggy paddle to where Santa waited. She inhaled a little bit of water while she was tried not to laugh, which went down the wrong tube. She spluttered as her feet found land, coughing painfully.

"See? Piece of cake," Santa pronounced as Kyra pulled herself onto the small island's shore, coughing. In hindsight, it should have been obvious to her the protection the dagger had provided disappeared the moment the *nuanai* had grabbed it from her. She also knew just how lucky she was to be as close to the shore as she had been. Beside her Georgie appeared to be in good shape. He continued to tug on her arm with his claws, trying to get her fully out of the water. Confused, Kyra crawled further up onto the sand. Her fuzzy robe was thoroughly soaked and waterlogged, as well as covered in a fine layer of sand. Her shoes were soaked as well.

"Yeah, sure," Kyra grunted as she turned over onto her back. The pearl in her pocket was still there, and she was surprised to find that while the fishmen had gone after the sword, they had left her and the pearl earring escape from their clutches. She reached into her pocket and pulled it out. As earlier, it was cool to the touch, but not unpleasant. She looked up at Santa. "That was *easy?*"

Her fingers uncurled from the pearl and for a brief instant the light of the moon above flashed off of its smooth surface. In the moonlit pearl Kyra thought she saw something. A figure, maybe. She wasn't too certain. There had been another image as well.

This one she recognized immediately, since her parents always had bonfires going in the backyard firepit during the summer and fall. It was a wall of flames.

A fine mist encircled the pearl and it slowly began to evaporate into the moonlight. Kyra watched, fascinated, as the mist curled upwards and strove towards the moon. In her mind she could see the moon goddess smiling at her.

Thank you, keiki, a fleeting ghost of a whisper danced across the breeze. Kyra's eyes burned as tears threatened to spill forth. There was an ethereal beauty to the moon goddess and her presence. Knowing she would never get to meet the moon goddess again hurt her heart. It was a good ache, but still a pain she did not fully expect.

Sniffling, she half-turned and tried to compose herself. It only took a few moments before she was okay. Turning, she informed Santa he had lost the small magical sword.

"You lost the *tanto*?" Santa asked her before shrugging. "Oh well. It served its purpose, I suppose. It's fortunate that you were so close to the island when you lost it."

"I'm soaked though," Kyra complained as she struggled to her feet. Georgie made a noise at her, so she scooped him up into her arms. The kaiju snuggled into her neck and began to make a funny purring sound. Kyra turned and looked at Santa. "They were terrified of Georgie. He's the only reason I made it out of there."

"Well of course they were," Santa nodded sagely. "Georgie's species has eaten *nuanai* for millennia, and the fishmen have long memories."

"Eaten... wait, how big will Georgie get?" Kyra asked in confusion.

"Oh, two, three hundred feet tall," Santa replied calmly. "But don't worry. It'll take many years for that to happen. In one hundred years he might be as big as a car. Plenty of time."

"Oh my..." Kyra's voice trailed off as she looked down at Georgie. "He... he's like Gojira!"

"Ah, no. Well yeah, okay, maybe a little," Santa conceded with a shrug. He seemed surprisingly okay with the fact Kyra's baby kaiju could one day destroy cities. "But it's going to be a very long time before he's that big! Besides, I don't think his kind have ever eaten a city before. Maybe a village a few thousand years ago..."

"Let's get him home," Kyra said in a resigned voice as she shook her soggy clothing. "Ugh. Do you have any extra shirts? Or a robe?"

"Just hop in the sleigh, you'll dry out," Santa stated as he looked into the sky. He frowned. "Speaking of, where are those reindeer? I *told* them to stay close."

As if on cue, Santa's sleigh appeared in the sky above. Kyra shook her head and her wet hair slapped her in the face. Sighing, she waited for the reindeer to land.

"Trust me Kyra, it'll be smooth sailing from here," Santa promised her.

Somehow, Kyra doubted that it

would get any easier. Smooth sailing and Santa Claus did not seem to go with one another. Chaos and Santa might be a much better fit, she decided.

CHAPTER 8 – THE LIGHTS OF THE NORTH

Surprisingly, Santa's sleigh had some sort of onboard heater, so Kyra's clothing was perfectly dry by the time they arrived at the Isle of Monsters. Or rather, maybe she shouldn't have been surprised. Everything about the night seemed crazy and bizarre, so having some sort of magical heater inside a flying sleigh driven by Santa Claus actually made sense. Kyra rubbed her eyes and yawned. Either Santa's weirdness was rubbing off on her or she was learning to just accept it and move on.

Kyra's thoughts drifted back to the Hawaiian moon goddess. She was happy to help Hina, who was finally able to return to her home after so many years. It wasn't right to keep someone from going to their home. And though Hawaii was beautiful, Hina wanted to go back home. Kyra understood this. There were days while at camp she wanted to go home very much. To be kept away for years would be too much for her to cope with.

Kyra yawned again. She was utterly exhausted and they still had a good while until they reached the Isle of Monsters. Maybe she could take a quick nap before they arrived?

Surely Georgie would wake her up if something happened.

"No time for napping, Kyra," Santa told her just as she settled down. It was like he could read her mind sometimes. She lifted her head and looked over at Georgie, who was snoring softly on the seat next to her. *Lucky guy*, she thought as she blinked and rubbed her eyes.

"Why not?" Kyra asked. She was pooped and really just wanted a nap. Closing her eyes, she began to focus on her breathing. It usually was the best way for her to fall asleep in a hurry. Breathe in, slowly breathe out. She felt herself begin to drift away.

"Because the Aurora Borealis is out," Santa told her in a quiet voice. "And it is something everyone should see at least one time in their life."

Kyra's eyes popped back open and she sat up quickly. It *was* something on her father's bucket list of things he wanted to see in his life. His enthusiasm for life and all of its adventures had spilled over onto his children, though it was Kyra more than the twins who wanted to see the northern lights with her dad. They had even talked, though she doubted he was being serious, about taking a trip to Norway one year to see them in one of the fancy new see-through igloos.

Or is that place in Sweden, she wondered.

"I wish my dad could see this," she continued in a wistful tone. Her eyes watched the magnificent waves of light dance across the sky, the various green and purple hues changing position every few moments. It was stunning and made her eyes water a little from not blinking. Next to her, Georgie nestled against her and began his strange little purr. She sighed.

"It's caused by solar winds interacting with Earth's magnetic fields," Santa murmured. He chuckled. "Leave it to science to explain what looks very much like magic to those who don't know."

"It is magical," Kyra whispered as she watched the northern lights continue their intricate dance across the night sky. "Just because it can be explained by science doesn't mean it can't still be magic."

"Truer words have never been spoken," Santa said in a strange voice. Kyra looked over at him and saw something in his face.

He's sad, she realized. *But why?*

"I used to joke about how the spirit of Christmas will never die," he said as they continued to watch the lights in the sky. "I told everyone I knew that greed would never triumph over the spirit of giving, of what the season means to different people. Family, sharing, helping the needy, rejoicing and celebrating. Dōngzhi, Christmas, Hanukah... didn't matter what they called it. The *spirit* was there, and that was all which mattered. Humanity would never lose their way so long as they had that spark, the idea of humanity. But... I don't know how it happened, or why. Greed managed to sneak its way into humanity's everyday thinking. Now all you see on television is 'more more more', and that's all anybody cares about. The latest and the greatest, not the love and spirit which goes into the giving."

"That's not true," Kyra argued. "It's the giving that's important."

"I hope the rest of the world sees it the way you do, Kyra," Santa said as the sleigh began to descend slowly towards a large landmass far below. He looked back at her and grinned, his momentary sadness seemingly forgotten. "Ah, there we go! Buckle up! Looks like we found the Isle of Monsters!"

CHAPTER 9 – THE ISLE OF MONSTERS

It was much greener than Kyra expected it to be.

She never thought of herself as a science geek but as far as she knew, jungles weren't common in the far Arctic north. Yet as they landed in an open, grassy clearing on the island it quickly became apparent the rules of nature were conveniently ignored here. Which was confusing for her. Santa had stated earlier that he didn't break the laws of physics, only bent them a little, yet this large island somewhere in the waters above Alaska shattered everything Kyra thought she knew about how science worked.

"Santa? Where are we?"

"The Isle of Monsters," Santa proclaimed. Kyra rolled her eyes as he chuckled, pleased with his little joke. "*Isla del Monstruos*, as Pablo the reindeer would say."

"I know *that*," she replied in an irritated tone. She paused and considered. "I mean... wait, who's Pablo?"

"The Isle of Monsters is in the Chukchi Sea," Santa explained, a twinkle in his eye as he seemed to enjoy his own little joke. "There are geothermal ducts all throughout the island which allows it to stay green and warm, even in the dead of winter. That's the science reason. There's also a magical one that I really don't understand too well."

"Of course," Kyra sighed. Santa had a weird way of following the laws of physics. Science was her thing, not magic. Even if she was traveling around the world in a sleigh with Santa Claus.

"Pablo is a reindeer who helps me when I'm south of the border," Santa continued as the sleigh landed in an open grass clearing next to the sandy shore. Kyra looked around but all she could see was green. It was shocking at just how vibrant the greens were. She'd never seen anything like it in her life. Santa was continuing to talk, not noticing her wide eyes as she stared into the jungle which shouldn't exist. "Just like the song, you know? *When Santa goes to Mexico, he brings a reindeer called Pablo...*"

"I... don't even know," Kyra sighed. She looked over at Georgie, who seemed to be grinning at her. She scoffed and gave him a fake frown. "Oh, you think it's funny, do you?"

"Mrawp!"

"Traitor," she muttered but smiled anyway. The baby kaiju seemed to have her sense of humor.

Santa chuckled. "Well, let's go and find his family."

"Santa," Kyra asked as something the Hawaiian moon goddess had said earlier tickled the back of her mind.

"Didn't Hina say something about his species being extinct?"

"Did she now?" Santa's bushy eyebrows came together as he seemed to think about it. He shrugged his shoulders. "I don't recall. But sometimes people are wrong. Or goddesses, in this case."

"Yes, she did," Kyra said. "What happens if we don't find them? What if she's right?"

"I'm sure we can figure something out," Santa said as he hopped out of the sleigh and stretched his back. He grimaced and there was a distinct *pop!* which came from his back. "Oh! That smarts. I've been sitting still for too long."

Georgie bounded out of the sleigh and began to sniff the air. Kyra blinked as she wondered just why there was so much light in the sky. It looked like it was almost dawn but she knew that couldn't be possible. Santa had promised to get her back home before anybody noticed. If it was dawn this far west, then her parents had already found her bed empty. She was going to be in so much trouble.

"Magic?" she whispered. Probably. *Hopefully*, she thought as Georgie bumped against her leg. She reached down and scratched a spot just behind his nose horn that he seemed to like. He chirped a little and rubbed against her a little more forcefully. She smiled down at him. *He's too cute.* It was like owning a puppy which would one day grow big enough to destroy Seattle.

She wasn't sure how she felt about that.

"Ah! We might be able to find some help over that way," Santa said as he pointed into the surrounding forest. Kyra looked and saw nothing, though there seemed to be a heavy fog in the direction he pointed. "I thought I saw a village there when we were coming in for a landing."

"I missed that," Kyra admitted as she realized the fog was actually smoke. It wasn't what she remembered from seeing from the news about the big forest fires but she could tell this was darker than fog, though not by much. It moved across the treetops and out to the sea, though slow enough to be mistaken for something other than smoke. *My bad*, she thought as she looked back at Santa. "Think the villagers can help us?"

"We won't know until we ask,"

Santa said. He rubbed his hands together. "Warmer than I expected it to be."

"But you said..." Kyra's voice trailed off. She shook her head. "Magic and science, I know. Never mind. Let's go talk to the villagers."

"Keep Georgie close," Santa warned. Kyra glanced back towards where Santa had pointed earlier and saw her baby kaiju wandering off.

"Georgie!" Kyra called out. The tiny monster looked back at her, his black eyes wide. "Stay close."

"Mrawp!" Georgie chirped back. He kicked a small pebble towards the forest, obviously upset at not being able to wander off and explore. He reminded her of her brothers sometimes. "*Mraaaaawp...*"

"Don't take that tone with me," Kyra told him as she got closer. She paused and frowned. "Wow. I sounded just like my mom when she's dealing with Jayden and Aiden."

"It happens to the best of us," Santa said in an amused tone. "We all end up sounding like our parents."

"You have a mom?" Kyra asked, surprised. Santa grinned.

"Of course I do," came the response. "I didn't just spring out of nothingness, you know. I'm not magic, the elves who work for me are."

"What was she like?" Kyra asked. "Is she still alive?"

"Ho ho ho!" Santa laughed. "This adventure we're on isn't about jolly old Nick, Kyra. Let's stick to the story of the little girl who is trying to save Christmas, and find her pet kaiju's family."

"Right," Kyra nodded. Between saving Christmas - though she didn't know what she was saving Christmas *from*, but knew it always tied into the adventure - and all which had happened since she first capture Santa in the tinsel trap, she needed to remember why she snuck out of her house in the first place. They needed to find Georgie his homes. If they failed, then her breaking the rules would mean she risked getting grounded for the rest of her life for nothing.

"Funny thing, though," Santa murmured as he looked into the jungle forest at the edge of the clearing. "I've never delivered presents here before."

"Why is that funny?" Kyra asked.

"It doesn't matter what culture it is," Santa explained as they began to walk in the direction of the slow-moving smoke. "Everyone has a practice of celebrating during this time of year. Kwanzaa, Saturnalia, Winter Solstice, Christmas, Hanukkah, Shab-e Yalda… they all celebrate with family, which brings about giving and feasting. The spirit is there in all but name. Because of this spirit, I get to go everywhere, and know everyone. But… I've never been here before."

"Maybe they don't celebrate?" Kyra asked, confused. She had never heard of half the holidays Santa had just named.

"I have never met a culture in history who did not celebrate the coming of winter, or celebration of the harvest," Santa said as he shrugged his shoulders. "Well, there was that one time in Chile, but that was a mix-up due to their winters being in June..."

The two paused as they could hear some sort of strange sound up ahead. It almost sounded like traffic but Kyra knew it couldn't be that. If it wasn't the sound of cars running, then what could it be? She looked over at Santa for answers.

For once, Santa did not seem to have any kind of immediate answer. He shrugged his shoulders and smiled. "Magic?" He offered.

It made as much sense as anything else, Kyra thought. Flying reindeer? Magic. Santa Claus coming down a chimney? Magic. Delivering presents around the world in one night?

Well, that could be quantum teleporting, Kyra allowed as she remembered an old science fiction show her parents loved. She had watched the reruns with them one time and really didn't get it. Then again, there were a lot of shows her parents watched and liked that she couldn't even understand.

"Magic works for me," Kyra grunted. It worked as well as anything else which had happened during the night. "It still sounds like traffic or something to me."

"Maybe it's a crowd of people?" Santa suggested.

"Never heard a crowd of people sound like cars and stuff before," Kyra said. Santa smirked.

"You've obviously never been to

Cairo the week before Ramadan," he said. "Well, I guess this is as good of a time as any to let you know this isn't how I saw tonight going."

"I didn't think the tinsel would work," Kyra pointed out.

"It's was a clever trap," Santa stated.

"Thanks for letting me come and help you save Christmas," Kyra said. She meant it, too. Everything she had done up to this point was something she never thought possible. Everything she thought she knew about the world was different now. It was scary, and yet amazing as well.

"Anytime," he said and straightened his coat. "Ready to go meet the natives?"

"I guess," Kyra said and they stepped into the jungle to track down the island's residents. Santa gave her a wide and encouraging smile.

"You know what? From here on out, I think everything is going to work out just fine."

CHAPTER TEN – THE LITTLE CITY OF NOWHERE

It took them less than ten minutes to find the village. Between the singing and the lights, the dense jungle foliage could not hide the village from them forever.

Georgie seemed to have no problem navigating through the jungle's undergrowth, picking his way through and around the worst of the trees thanks to his small size. Kyra had a few problems but it helped she didn't have a bulky winter coat on. Santa, however...

Kyra looked back as Santa's oversized red coat became stuck on yet another branch of a tree. After a few interesting words in languages Kyra didn't really think she should know, Santa finally managed to become unstuck for the fourth time in as many minutes. Grinning in embarrassment, he offered a weak explanation.

"Uh... I don't trek through jungles often."

"Costa Rica is a jungle," Kyra reminded him.

"Different rules, different outfit," Santa said. He tugged at his heavy red overcoat as they pushed through the final cluster of vines hanging from one of the jungle trees. "This isn't what I wear anywhere near the equator."

"Uh, Santa?" Kyra's eyes went wide as she saw the village for the first time. "I thought you said this was a small village?"

"It is," Santa said before pausing and looking up. His bushy eyebrows went even higher. "Well... that's interesting."

Standing before them was a large street with traffic and everything. Across the busy road was a tall skyscraper, something straight out of a massive metropolis like New York or Chicago. There were smaller buildings all around as well, and each one was filled with a massive number of shoppers filing in and out. There were lines around the block and massive electronic billboards atop each roof.

Every single person who came and went from the stores hand their hands filled with oversized shopping bags. They were all in a hurry and pushing past one another. Nobody was wishing one another season's greetings of any kind. Not Merry Christmas, Happy Hanukkah, nothing. It was clearly Christmas Eve in this strange place, though something about it all bugged Kyra. She looked at Santa, who bore a very confused look on his face.

"They're obviously getting gifts for one another," he said as he watched the moving crowds. "But I've never been drawn here. I saw a small village from the sky and yet, this is a good-sized city. You're telling me that on an Arctic Island in the middle of a frozen sea there's a bustling metropolis?"

"Magic?" Kyra offered. Santa looked at her and chuckled slightly.

"I knew that explanation would come back to haunt me," Santa proclaimed. He glanced back at the throngs of people, still confused. "I don't understand it though. How does this work?"

"Greed," a sinister whisper suggested from the jungle canopy behind them. Kyra yelped and whirled around, startled. Georgie growled and snapped at the unseen darkness while Santa merely rolled his eyes and sighed heavily. The voice continued. "This is my power, my control. They buy gifts because they have to, not because they want them to mean anything. It's a competition to get the latest and greatest gift. This is humanity's future. It's coming, Saint

Nick. I told you this before."

"And I've told you many times that the human spirit won't be so easily lured into this loss of itself," Santa countered. "Kyra, I'd like to introduce you to an old friend of mine. Kyra, this is Mr. Troubadour. Troubadour, meet Kyra."

"Uh... hi?" Kyra offered. She gasped as the darkness came together within the jungle and began to form a solid shape.

Out of these gathered shadows stepped a thin man in a dark business suit. His face was narrow and lean, his eyes were bright in the darkness. Troubadour looked like the typical businessman to Kyra. Her father dealt with enough of them from his consulting firm and she'd seen quite a few men who looked almost exactly like Troubadour come and go.

"Look at them," Troubadour said and waved a hand in the direction of the shoppers. "Coming, going. Always in a hurry to the next sale, always in a rush to buy the latest and greatest doodad. It's all about the gift, the present, the excitement about what is inside the specially wrapped box. Open the present, toss the gift aside, and move on to the next. This is the way here, and will be across the entire world in the morning. Just watch."

"You're wrong," Kyra shocked herself by arguing with the terrifying man. "People love receiving gifts because of the meaning behind them!"

"Really?" Troubadour sneered at her. "Because I remember a very disappointed girl when she opened a box and found a cute, adorable baby kaiju instead of the dog she had asked for. I don't recall her being thankful for the fact her mother and father got her a gift. Can you tell me about this little girl, Kyra?"

"That was a cheap shot," Santa pointed out, his tone cross. "Really, Troubadour? Going to pick on a little girl?"

"No, he's right," Kyra said as she nodded. "I was surprised, and disappointed. But I was more shocked at *what* was in the box. I knew my mom and dad meant well, and I figured there'd been a mistake or something. I panicked, and one thing my dad always says is to never panic. I was wrong, but I'm not wrong now. This isn't Christmas at all. What you have here isn't Christmas, or any of the other holidays."

"Says one little voice in the sea of humanity," Troubadour said.

"Sometimes it only takes one," Kyra said loudly. A few of the people walking along the street had paused and were looking at the trio now, curious expressions on their faces.

"Mrawp!" Georgie agreed. Kyra bent down and scooped him up. He butted his head against her shoulder. His horn thumped her but it didn't hurt. She was going to have to teach him how to properly cuddle in the future so he wouldn't hurt her, Kyra thought.

Suddenly it dawned on her that she wasn't thinking about life after Georgie any longer. She looked down at her little bundle of kaiju and smiled. Georgie, like any other pet, wasn't something to get rid of when it started being a problem. He, and all the other pets in the world, was special.

"My mom and dad got me Georgie because they loved me," Kyra said. "Well, they got me a dog, and Santa swapped Georgie in his place. Maybe... Santa loved Georgie and wanted him to have a good home, so he gave him to me? It's not the cost of the gift, though. It's the idea of giving. It doesn't matter how little the present costs, right? It's about the emotion behind it! That's what my Nana Madeira always said. It's the love, not the present."

"You see, Troubadour? The one spark in the darkness can light the way," Santa said. He waved his hand towards the crowd which had been watching them. "The one tiny little voice has been heard."

"This year? Sure," Troubadour said as he melted back into the shadows. "Next year? The year after?"

"Then I'll say it again and again until everyone hears!" Kyra shouted into the dark. "The spirit of the season is family and love! Sharing and giving! Just because you can buy something doesn't make it special. It has to mean something!"

"You know, Kyra? You may have just saved Christmas," Santa murmured as the onlookers began to whisper amongst themselves. He looked at her and Georgie and smiled. "It also looks like you made a decision."

"I did," she agreed. "Georgie is coming home with me. I… I'll figure out a way to explain to my parents why we need to keep him safe."

"You know, Kyra, sometimes people see what they expect to see," Santa said as his sleigh suddenly appeared overhead. It settled down on the sidewalk, which cause even more people to stop and stare. "Take all of them, for example. They weren't expecting to be in the middle of a magical story like this, I'm pretty sure. They'll explain it away later and, in time, their memory of this night will change. Just like yours, Kyra."

"No," she said. "I'll never forget this night."

"No, not with Georgie around," Santa agreed. He hopped into his sleigh. "Let's go, Kyra. We have to get you home."

Holding Georgie tightly to her chest, Kyra climbed into the sleigh. She turned and looked at the crowd of people, who were still staring and whispering. She couldn't hear them, not really, but she could feel the air change. An idea had been put in each of their heads. The idea of gifting, not just buying. She could tell. It might not last, but for this year at least, Kyra knew Christmas would be okay.

The sleigh shot up off the ground and flew into the night. Kyra felt a wave of exhaustion wash over her. She curled up on the seat and pulled her robe tighter. Georgie began his strange little purr and she rubbed his nose. She was tired from all of their adventures from the night.

"Just a quick nap, Santa," Kyra said sleepily as she closed her eyes.

"Go ahead," Santa agreed. "You earned it. And Kyra?"

"Hmmm?"

"Merry Christmas."

"Merry Christmas, Santa," Kyra managed before she began to softly snore.

"Kyra?"

"Are we there yet, Santa?"

"Kyra, it's time to wake up."

Wait a second. That wasn't Santa's voice.

"Ugh..." she grunted and rubbed her eyes. Sunlight was streaming into her bedroom through the window. Kyra was in her bed and not in Santa's sleigh. There was no sign of anything out of the ordinary. Somehow, in spite of everything she had done the night before with Santa, she felt rested. What should have taken days had been accomplished in minutes. *Unless it had all been a dream*, she thought. *Was I dreaming? Was it?*

Pushing her blanket off the bed, Kyra rolled her feet to the floor and found Georgie sound asleep on her shoes. She smiled. The adventures they had the night before weren't a dream. They'd been real, which meant she had met Santa. Her and Georgie *had* saved Christmas, and shown the spirit of giving to the strange people on the Isle of Monsters. And they had made it back without anybody catching her, though she did not know how she had gotten back into her bed. *Magic*, she thought as she imagined Santa's laughter.

"Your brothers have been very patient waiting for you to get up for presents," her father said as he looked down at Georgie, who was yawning and stretching out. The red kaiju was still a baby, but fully extended with his tail he was about the same size as Romeo. Her father grinned at the sight. "I'm glad to see you like your dog. What made you change your mind?"

"My... dog?" she asked, confused for a moment until she recalled Santa's parting words back on the island. *People see what they expect to see*, she thought. "Oh. You mean Georgie. Right. I like him a lot. He's friendly and I think we're going to be just fine."

"Good," her father said as he walked out of the room. "Hmmm... Romeo and Georgie. Odd couple of names but hey, who am I to judge? Not sure about letting him sleep in your room yet, since he's probably not potty trained, but that's a discussion for later. Hurry up. I doubt the twins are going to be able to wait much longer. Plus, after presents we're making waffles."

Kyra waited a moment before she slid off her bed fully and sat next to Georgie. The kaiju's tail was wagging, just like a dog's would, and he seemed genuinely pleased. Kyra scratched his head just behind his horns.

"We did it, Georgie," Kyra sighed and leaned against her stout companion. "We saved Christmas, and thanks to Santa people won't see a baby kaiju but a small dog. You think anyone will notice when they pet you?"

"Mrawp!" Georgie chirped and she laughed.

"No, I don't think so either." She clambered to her feet and scooped Georgie up and into her arms. She rested her cheek against his warm scaly skin for a moment before looking into his bright eyes. "C'mon, let's do presents and then eat."

Kyra and Georgie headed downstairs. She knew their first adventure was over, but there would be many more to come. First, however, they needed to make it through Christmas morning.

"Merry Christmas, Georgie," she told the kaiju as he nudged her shoulder. He did his strange little purr, which made her smile. "Let's open some presents, big guy."

"Mrawp!" Georgie agreed.

THE END

A finalist of multiple literary awards, Jason Cordova was a pretty good kid who never snuck out at night to try and capture Santa Clause, nor did he ever have a pet kaiju. He does have a few cats and lives in Virginia, though, which is almost as unusual since he was born in California a long time ago. When he's not writing books, he coaches youth basketball.

If you would like to know more about him, please visit www.jasoncordova.com. However, be warned: sometimes he gets carried away on his website and starts blathering about odd things using very... colorful language that your parents wouldn't want you to use.

Made in the USA
Coppell, TX
04 December 2021

67099054R00109